Spaghetti AND Meatball

WRITTEN BY
Meredith Lesney

ILLUSTRATED BY
Felicia Parish

Printed in the United States of America

Cover and interior design by Bravura Graphics, LLC.

Library of Congress information available upon request.

ISBN 978-0-9986531-2-9

2 4 6 8 10 9 7 5 3 1 paperback

To my loving parents, Suzie and Chas:
Thank you for teaching me what unconditional love is!
–ML

To Weston and Isaiah, who make me laugh every day!
–FP

A special thanks to Danielle and Josh at Bravura Graphics!

Thank you to Joanna Lemay for being the best proofreader ever!

Rriiiiiiiiiiiiiiiiing!

"Oh my goodness. The day is over!" said Mrs. Sandwich. She was Socken Valley's school librarian.

"Boys and girls, please finish checking out your books. It's time to return to your class and go home for the day."

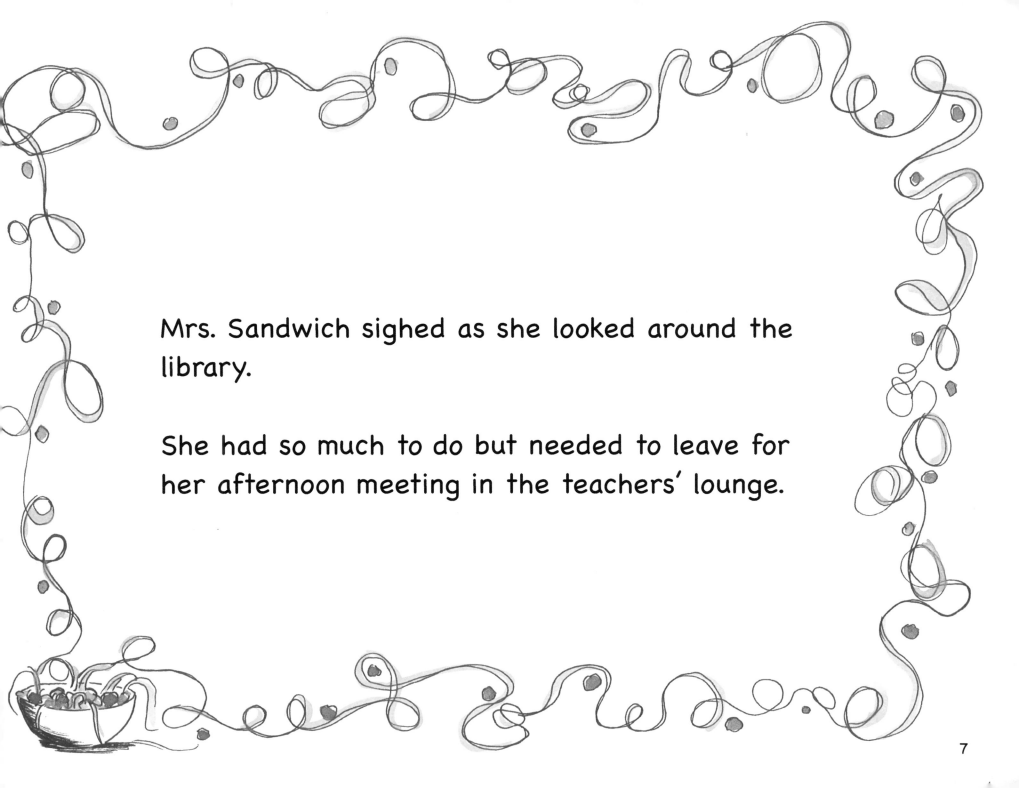

Mrs. Sandwich sighed as she looked around the library.

She had so much to do but needed to leave for her afternoon meeting in the teachers' lounge.

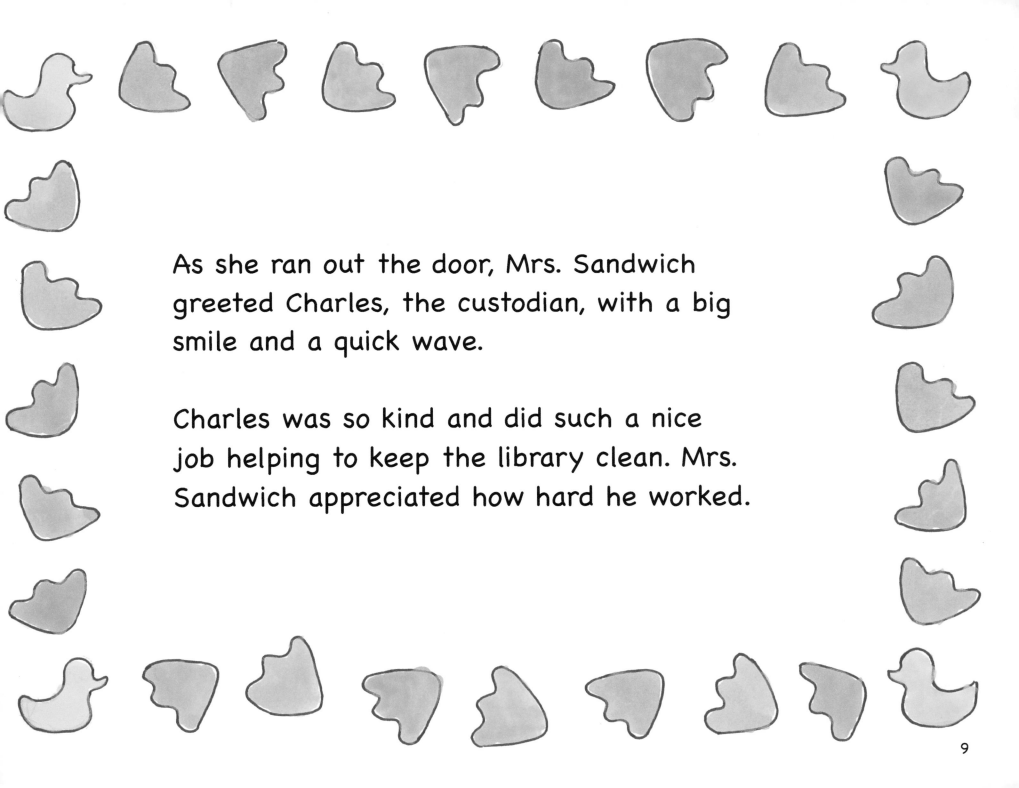

As she ran out the door, Mrs. Sandwich greeted Charles, the custodian, with a big smile and a quick wave.

Charles was so kind and did such a nice job helping to keep the library clean. Mrs. Sandwich appreciated how hard he worked.

Charles loved to listen to music and dance around while he cleaned.

He started cleaning up the library, and as he danced, he mistakenly bumped into a box of old books that someone had just donated.

Charles finished up and left the library. He didn't notice the box of books that spilled onto the floor.

"Heh-woah? Is anyone out there?"

A thin, flat, yellow duck climbed out of one
of the books that Charles had knocked over.

The duck was very hungry and tired,
because he had been stuck in that book
for a very long time.

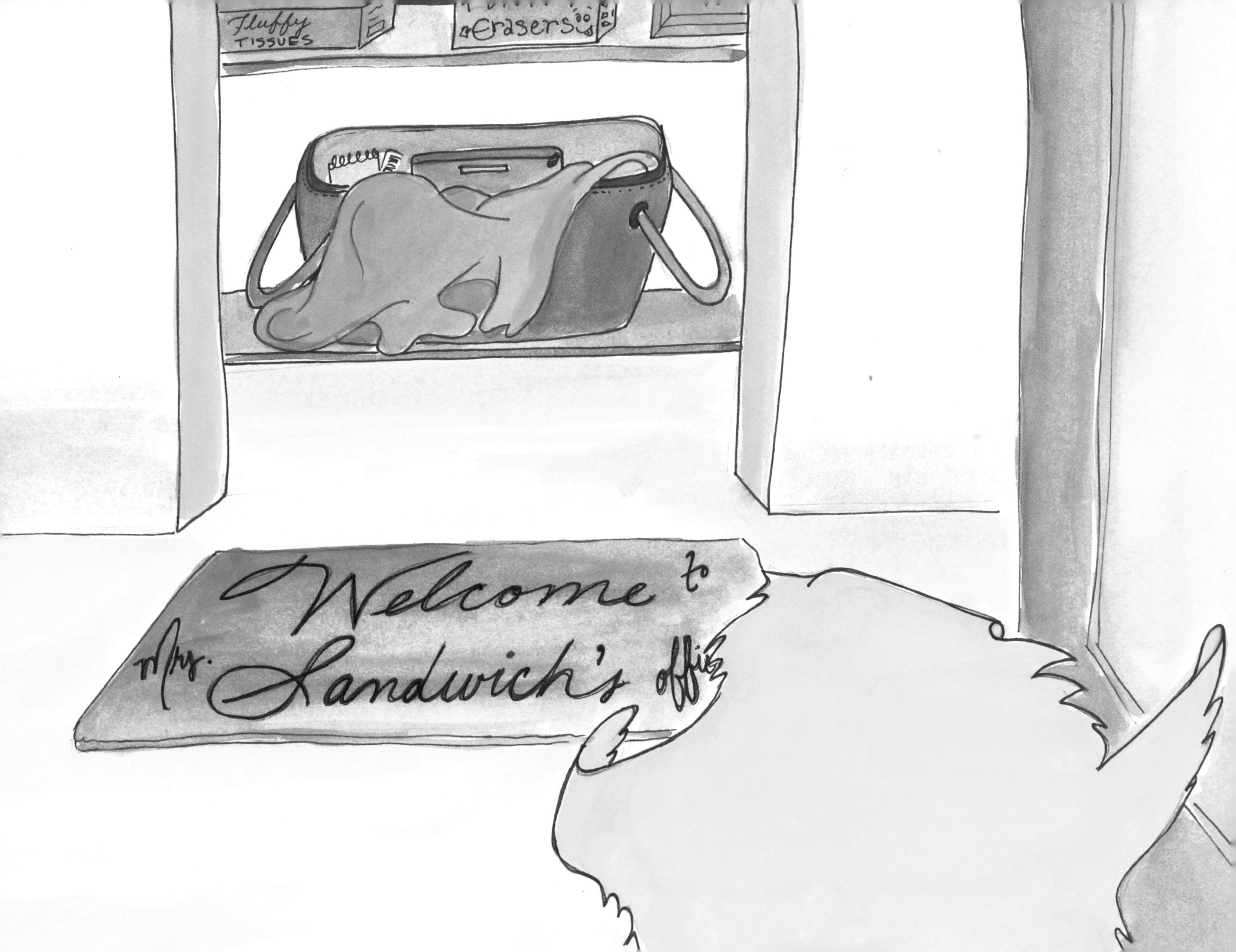
Fluffy TISSUES
Erasers
Welcome to
Mrs. Landwich's offi

The duck tried to walk but kept tipping over.

He didn't know what to do until he saw what looked like a soft blanket.

He crawled over and snuggled into that nice, soft blanket and fell fast asleep.

A minute later, Mrs. Sandwich rushed through the door. She was relieved that it was finally time to go home.

She grabbed her purse and hurried on her way. Mrs. Sandwich was excited because it was spaghetti night.

She loved spaghetti! She couldn't wait to get home to start cooking.

At home, Mrs. Sandwich set her bag down on the kitchen table as she hurried to grab her apron so she could start cooking.

When she bent over to grab some tomatoes out of the refrigerator, she heard a small voice.

"Heh-woah."

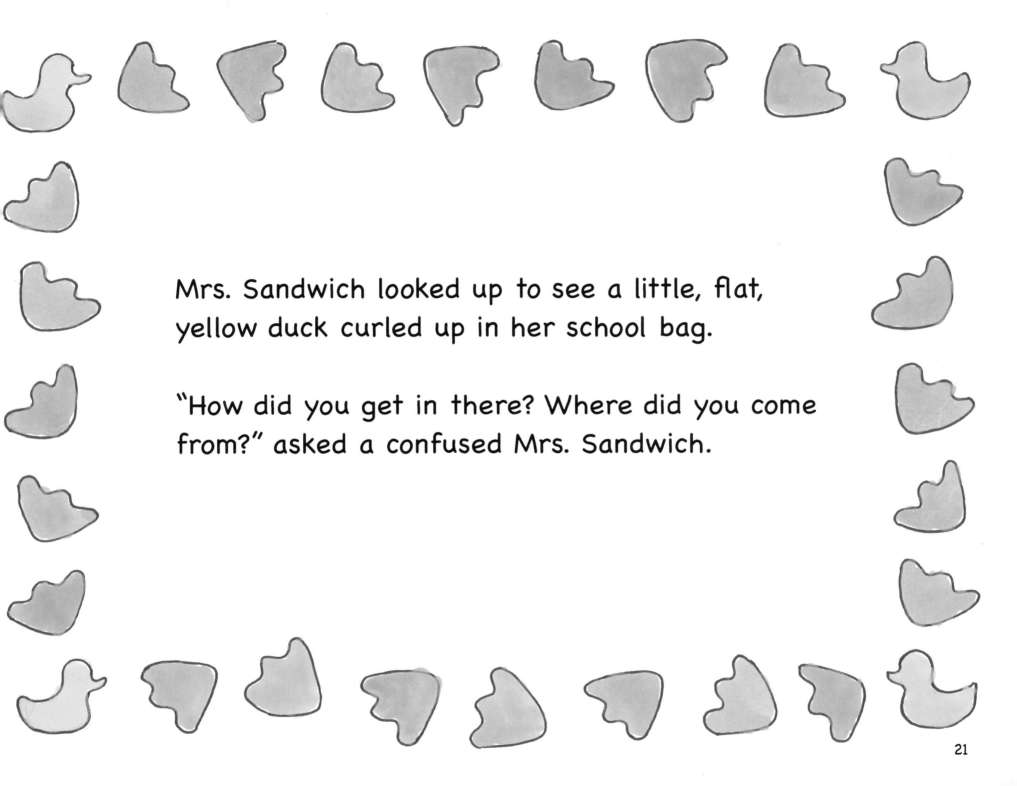

Mrs. Sandwich looked up to see a little, flat, yellow duck curled up in her school bag.

"How did you get in there? Where did you come from?" asked a confused Mrs. Sandwich.

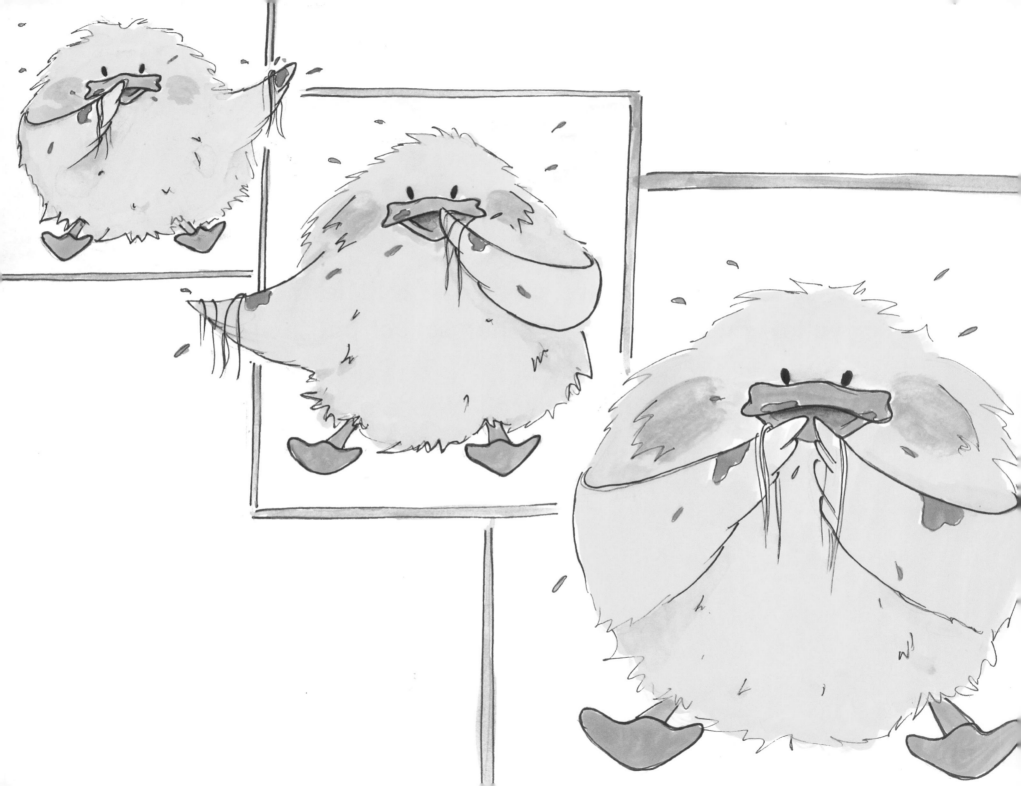

The little duck tried to talk but was just too tired and hungry.

Mrs. Sandwich realized this, quickly cooked her famous spaghetti, and gave the duck a big plateful.

As the duck was eating, Mrs. Sandwich realized he was getting fluffier and fluffier and rounder and rounder.

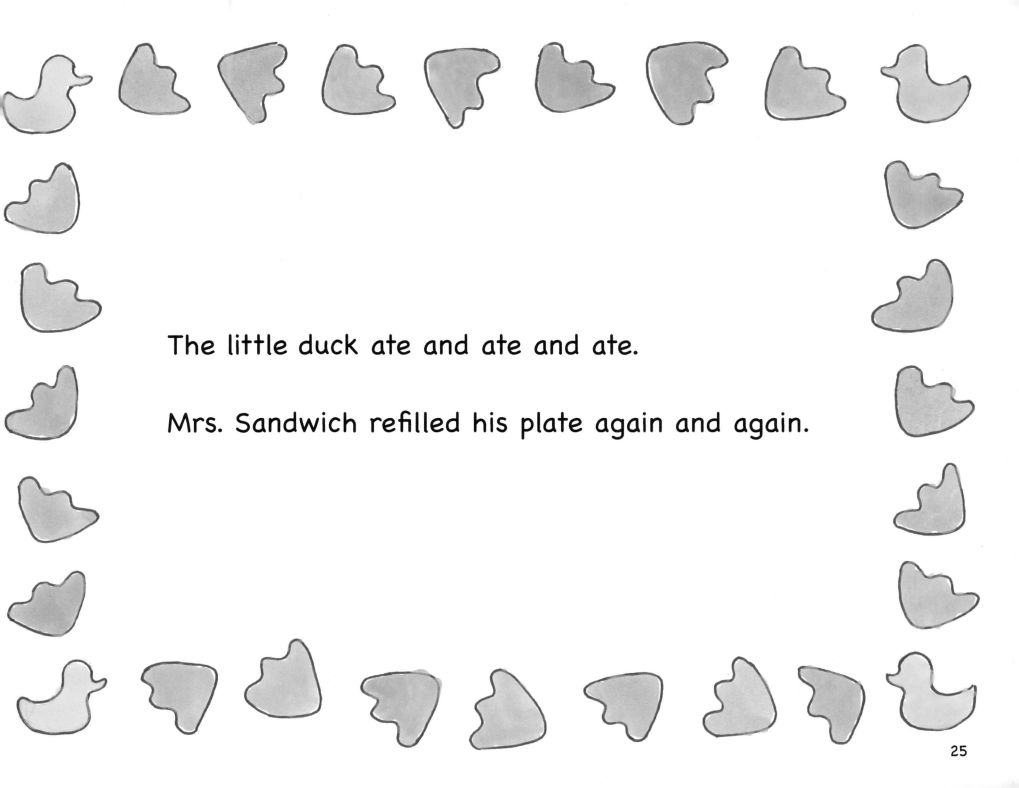

The little duck ate and ate and ate.

Mrs. Sandwich refilled his plate again and again.

Mrs. Sandwich asked the duck what his name was. The now large, round, yellow duck looked confused.

"I don't have a name," he said through mouthfuls of spaghetti. "What's your name?"

"Well my name is Shelly, but everyone calls me Jelly because when I was younger my sister couldn't say Shelly. She called me Jelly, and it just stuck."

"Can you give me a name?" the duck asked.

Mrs. Sandwich took one look at the duck covered in spaghetti sauce.

Laughing, she said, "Your new name should be Meatball because you look like a meatball all covered with sauce and spaghetti. Where did you come from?"

"I don't know," said the yellow duck. "I fell out of a book. I lived in there, and that is all I can remember. Can you help me find a home? I don't want to go back into the book. It was so lonely in there."

After dinner, Mrs. Sandwich gave Meatball a bath and cleaned him all up.

She read him stories, made him hot chocolate, colored with him, and gave him lots of hugs.

Meatball loved it.

Meatball was very curious and asked, "Why are you sharing all of these things with me?"

Mrs. Sandwich replied, "That is how you show love. When you care about people, you are kind and nice to them. You do things for them that make their hearts happy!"

Suddenly, Meatball had a good idea!

He gave Mrs. Sandwich an extra big hug and hurried out of the room.

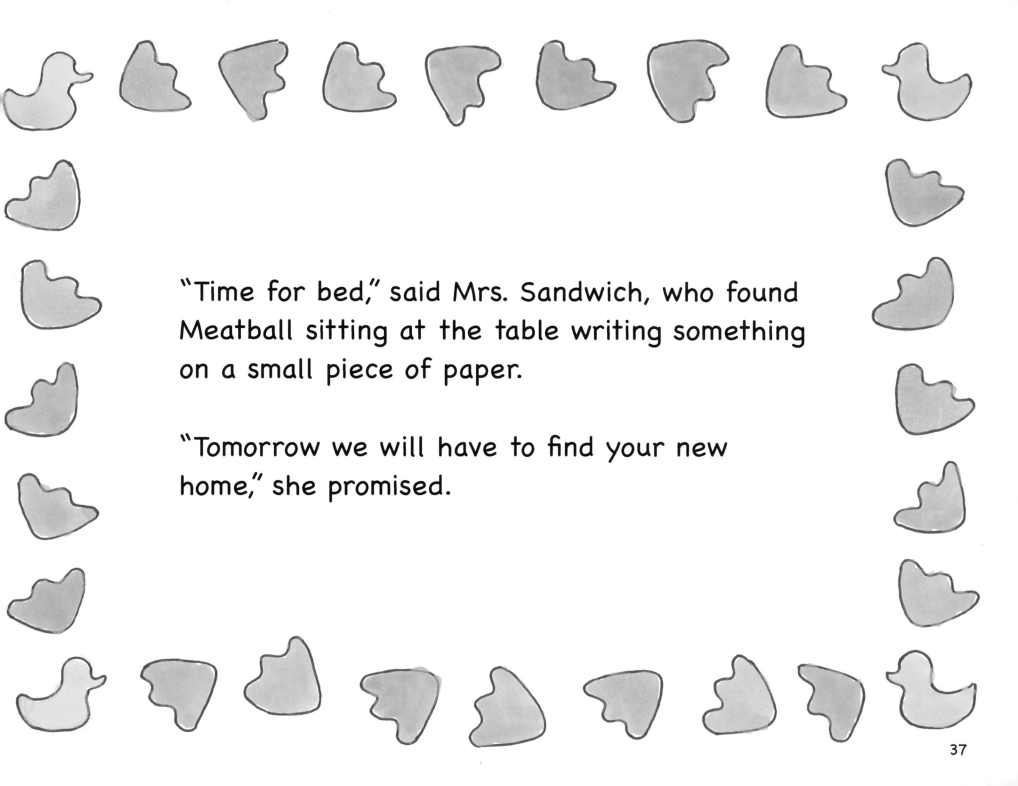

"Time for bed," said Mrs. Sandwich, who found Meatball sitting at the table writing something on a small piece of paper.

"Tomorrow we will have to find your new home," she promised.

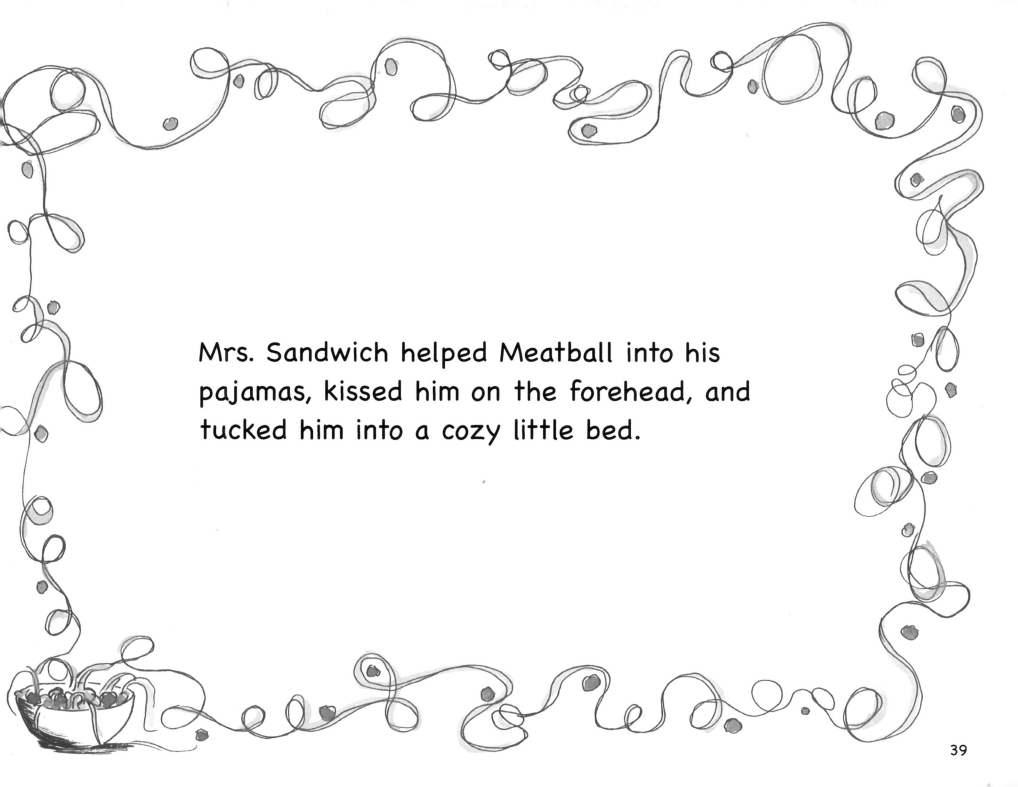

Mrs. Sandwich helped Meatball into his pajamas, kissed him on the forehead, and tucked him into a cozy little bed.

As Mrs. Sandwich was sliding into her own bed, she found a clump of cold spaghetti and a crumpled-up piece of paper beneath her pillow.

It read, " Will you be my Mommy? I want to be your Meatball Sandwich."

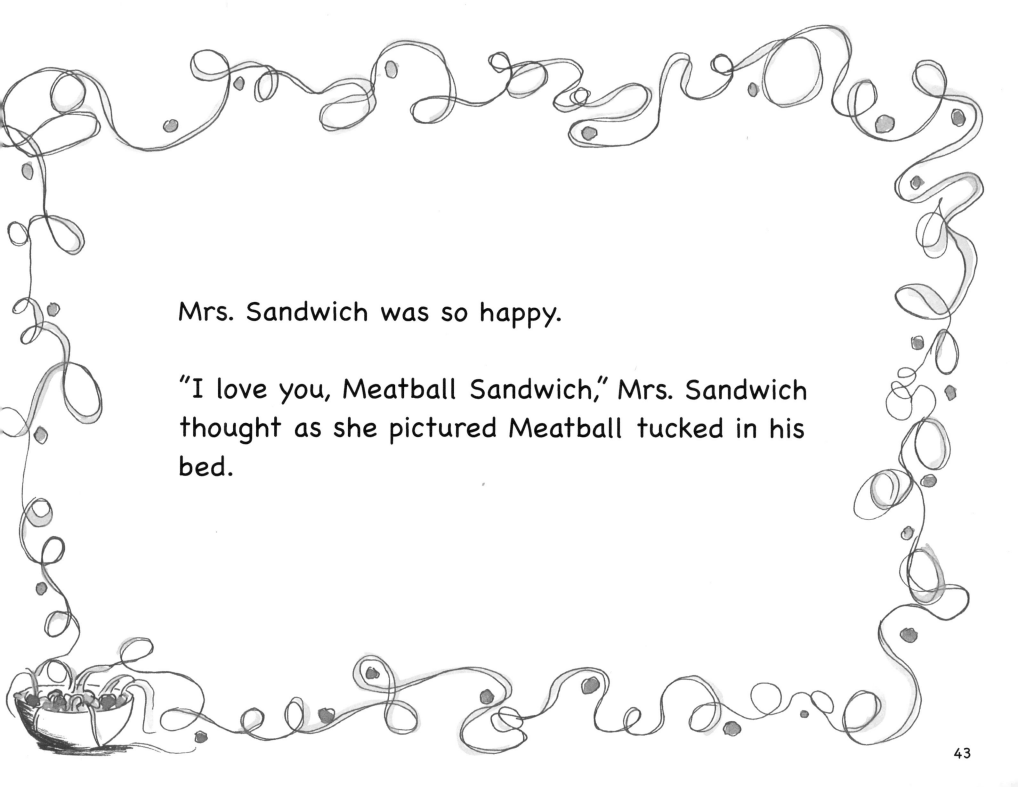

Mrs. Sandwich was so happy.

"I love you, Meatball Sandwich," Mrs. Sandwich thought as she pictured Meatball tucked in his bed.

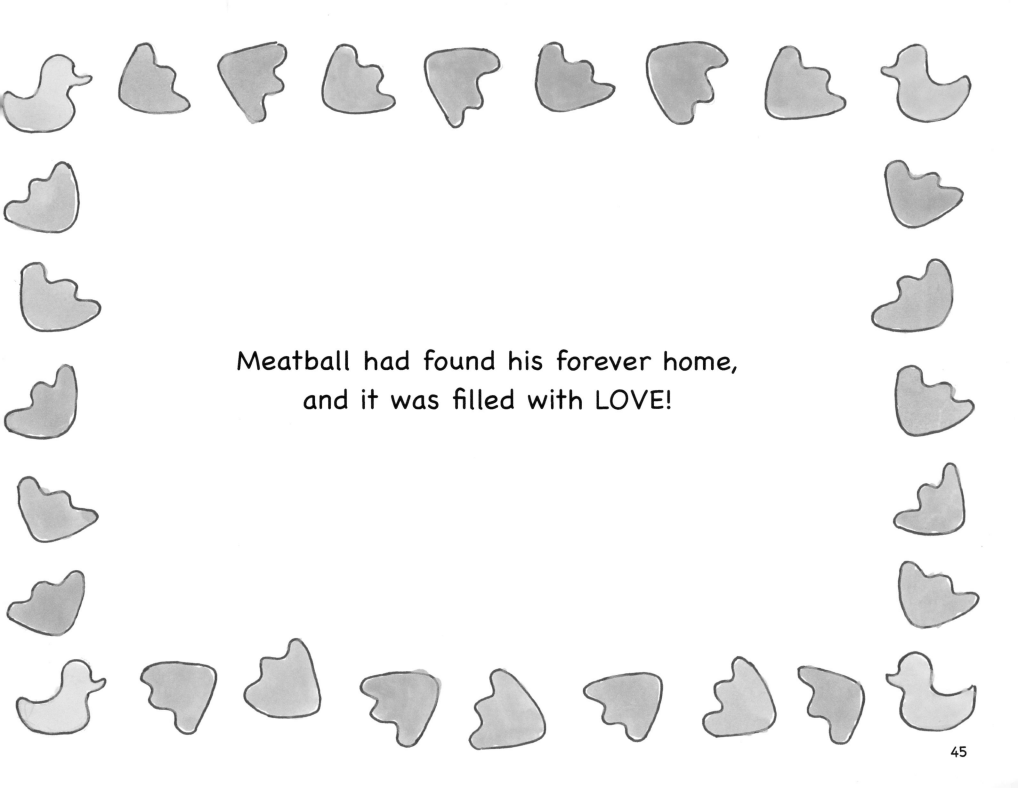

Meatball had found his forever home,
and it was filled with LOVE!

KIDS' CREATIONS

Meatball

Hi!!

Cayden 5

46

Meatball

SANDWICH

Meatball is

AMAZIng

meat ball

meat ball

meat ball ♡

KIDS' CREATIONS

Stay Tuned

for more adventures!

CPSIA information can be obtained
at www.ICGtesting.com
Printed in the USA
BVHW090931290919
559679BV00001BA/2/P

9 780999 865312 9